W9-AOZ-615

CAPTAiN
☆WESOME
TaKes a Dive

By STAN KIRBY

Illustrated by
GEORGE O'CONNOR

LITTLE SIMON

New York   London   Toronto   Sydney   New Delhi

LITTLE SIMON

An imprint of Simon & Schuster Children's Publishing Division • 1230 Avenue of the Americas, NewYork, NewYork 10020 • Copyright © 2012 by Simon & Schuster, Inc. All rights reserved, including the right of reproduction in whole or in part in any form. LITTLE SIMON is a registered trademark of Simon & Schuster, Inc., and associated colophon is a trademark of Simon & Schuster, Inc. For information about special discounts for bulk purchases, please contact Simon & Schuster Special Sales at 1-866-506-1949 or business@simonandschuster.com. The Simon & Schuster Speakers Bureau can bring authors to your live event. For more information or to book an event contact the Simon & Schuster Speakers Bureau at 1-866-248-3049 or visit our website at www.simonspeakers.com. Manufactured in the United States of America 0412 FFG • First Edition 10 9 8 7 6 5 4 3 2 1

Library of Congress Cataloging-in-Publication Data

Kirby, Stan. Captain Awesome takes a dive / by Stan Kirby ; illustrated by George O'Connor. — 1st ed. p. cm. — (Captain Awesome ; 4) Summary: To finish summer swimming lessons, Eugene brings out his superhero alter ego, Captain Awesome, to confront the "Blobby Blob-Blob" at the deep end of the pool. [etc.] [1. Superheroes—Fiction. 2. Swimming—Fiction. 3. Summer—Fiction.] I. O'Connor, George, ill. II. Title. PZ7.K633529Can 2012 [Fic]—dc23 2011023401

ISBN 978-1-4424-4202-3 (pbk)

ISBN 978-1-4424-4203-0 (hc)

ISBN 978-1-4424-4204-7 (eBook)

Table of Contents

CHAPTER 1

School's Out, Twist and Shout!

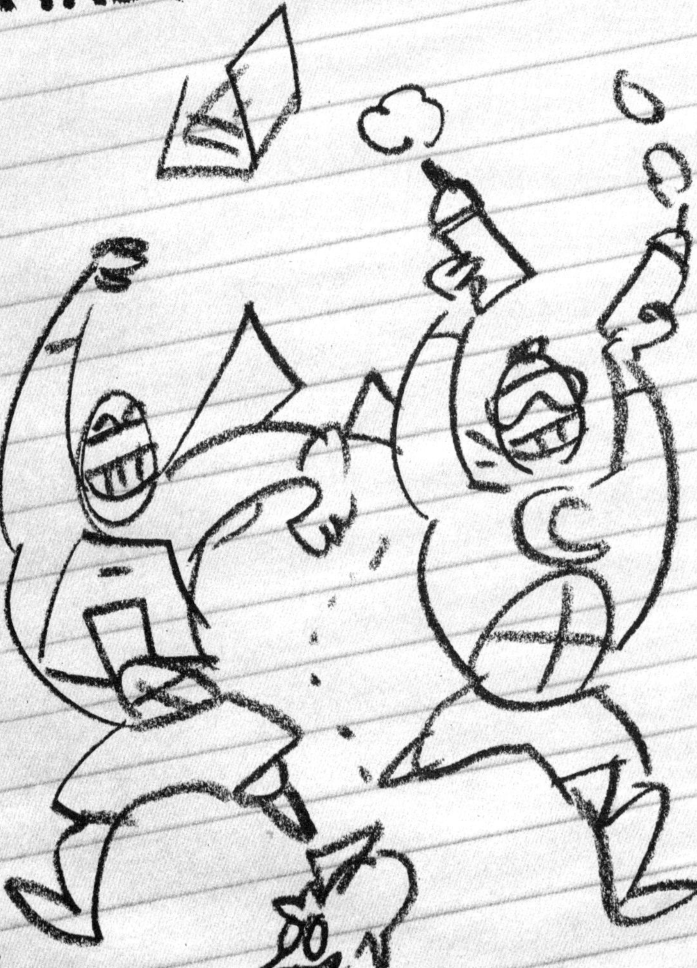

By Eugene

Could time go any s-l-o-w-e-r? When would summer vacation ever get here!?

Eugene McGillicudy sat at his desk in Ms. Beasley's class. His Super Dude Digital Command Watch counted down the remaining minutes.

What's that?!

You've never heard of Super Dude, the greatest, most powerful superhero on several planets?

The superhero who once defeated Mower Mouth, the big, mean-mouth Martian that devoured yards and soccer fields with its Mower Martian Mouth?

Without Super Dude's comic books, Eugene would never have become Captain Awesome or formed the Sunnyview Superhero Squad with his best friend, Charlie Thomas Jones, also known as . . . Nacho Cheese Man!

Only six more minutes—three hundred sixty seconds!—stood between Eugene and Charlie's seventy-one super summer days of fighting evil in Sunnyview. Not once would he have to hear things like his teacher saying, "Please take your seats."

Eugene had even made a list of his summer plans:

1. Learn to be the best swimmer ever.

2. Sleep as late as possible.

3. Stop evil from eviling.

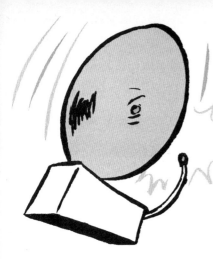

DING-DING-
ABING-BING!

THAT WAS THE BELL!

FINALLY!

SUMMER! VACATION! HAD! OFFICIALLY! BEGUN!

Eugene rocketed to his cubby. "Let's go, Charlie!"

Aside from putting evil on an asteroid prison orbiting the twin moons of See Ya Later, is there anything better than summer vacation? Eugene sure didn't think so.

Charlie packed up his cheese

containers from his cubby and stuffed them in his backpack. Nacho Cheese Man's Dairy Defense couldn't be left at school for the entire summer. There's no telling what bad guys would do if they got their evil hands on the cheesy goodness of Hot Jalapeño Surprise or Titanic Taco Blast.

Plus the expiration dates were in July.

"See ya later, My! Me! Mine! Mere-DITH!" Eugene said and waved to Meredith Mooney.

Meredith stuck up her nose and stomped out of the class.

"No school, no homework, and no Meredith for a whole summer!" Charlie cheered. "I don't know which one I'll miss the *least*."

Eugene picked up Turbo's ball. After all, superheroes can't go on patrol without their trusty hamster sidekicks. All three left the classroom.

It was time for one last school patrol!

Eugene and Charlie headed down the hall. Lockers were open, papers were scattered everywhere. It looked like Messypotamian, the slobby villain who never cleaned

his room, had returned to mess up
the school.

"Evil sounds from the cafeteria!" Charlie gasped.

The boys raced to the lunch-
room, flung open the doors, and
saw true evil.

The two boys dove for cover.

"It's our old enemy, Dr. Yuck
Spinach!" Eugene whispered.

"He must've escaped from
Asteroid Prison and returned to

continue his evil vegetable plans!"

"There's only one way out of this veggie trap—" Eugene said. "A direct charge through Dr. Spinach's Cafeteria Lair."

"That's insane!" Charlie gasped. "We will never make it! He'll use his Okra Bombs and Asparagus Spears!"

"Yes. And his Parsnips of Doom, too," Eugene replied. "But Super Dude never says never!"

It's time for action!

"CHAAAAARGE!" he shouted and raced into the cafeteria!

Oops!

Eugene tripped over the door-way and flopped to the floor.

ROLL!

Turbo's plastic ball flew from Eugene's hands and rolled across the cafeteria floor . . . stopping at Dr. Spinach's feet.

"EEEPS!" Charlie gasped in horror as Dr. Spinach turned to pick up Turbo.

"What have we here?" the evil chef of leafy green yuckiness growled.

Eugene and Charlie yanked their costumes from their backpacks.

"Don't touch my sidekick!" Captain Awesome yelled in his evil-fighting voice.

"You shall not harm Turbo on this day, Dr. Yuck Spinach! Not if Captain Awesome and I, Nacho Cheese Man, have anything to say about it!" Nacho Cheese Man shouted in his evil-fighting voice as well. Then, the superhero friends leaped into action.

CHAPTER 2

Danger Is a Wet and Stinky Diaper Queen

By Eugene

"**M**arco!" Eugene closed his eyes and called out across the pool, looking for Charlie.

"Polo!" Charlie called back. He floated like the Super Silent Crocodilios from Super Dude's Holiday Special No. 2.

It was Saturday, the first day of summer vacation, and Eugene and Charlie were splashing and swimming at the Sunnyview Community Center swimming pool. The sun was high in the sky and that made the water feel like a bath without soap.

The boys had been playing Marco Polo for only a few minutes when Charlie felt inspired. "Let's play Super Dude Polo!"

The rules of Super Dude Polo were from the Super Dude Summer Vacation Special No. 3. That comic was so rare, the only known copy was in the Super Dude Museum in

Blacksburg, Virginia. Fortunately, the rules were posted online!

Charlie had them memorized:

"The rules of Super Dude Polo are very simple. Player one closes his eyes and calls out the first half of a Super Dude villain's name. Player two, whose eyes are not closed, responds by saying the second half of the name, then tries to get away before player one can find him."

Eugene eagerly agreed and closed his eyes.

"Sir Stinky . . . !" Eugene called out.

"Stinkopotomus!" Charlie called back.

Eugene dove for the sound of Charlie's voice, but Charlie swam away laughing.

"Commander Barf . . . !" Eugene yelled.

"Pudding!!" Charlie replied,

clapping his hands.

Eugene jumped to the right, but Charlie wasn't there.

"Mr. Mad . . . !" Eugene called out once more.

"Haturday!"

Eugene was locked on to Charlie this time, but before Eugene could grab him, something brushed against his back.

BRUSH!

Was that Charlie horsing around, or was it something worse?

Eugene opened his eyes. It was worse.

Their most worstest enemy, Queen Stinkypants from the Planet Baby, bobbed up and down in her evil Giraffe Floatie! She unleashed the kicking power of her terrible Surprise Splash Attack!

"Look out!" Eugene pushed Charlie out of the way of incoming danger.

The water splashed in Eugene's face. "My eyes!" he yelped. "I'm soaked with watery evil!"

While Eugene rubbed the evil from his eyes, Charlie leaped into action.

"I'll put an end to this!" Charlie reached for a can of his powerful squirt cheese—but where was it?

Then he remembered! He'd left his cans on the side of the pool.

OOPS!

"Grble-drble! Grble-drble-drble!" Queen Stinkypants cackled and then unleashed the annoying power of her Baby Laugh. Eugene and Charlie covered each other's ears, then realized that wouldn't work and covered their own.

The Queen's Baby Laugh was much more than just annoying. It was a call that unleashed her wild

pack of hungry superhero-eating
Electric Piranha Sharks!

CHOMP!

"Time to give those sharks a
superhero meal with a side order
of butt-kicking!" Captain Awesome
announced.

He and Nacho Cheese Man
took a deep breath and started to
swim toward the chomping electric
fish . . . .

CHAPTER 3

Don't Trust a Dude with a Whistle

By
Eugene

*B*REET-TWEET-TWEET!

Eugene heard the whistle first. Was it an alarm? A secret signal? Was Queen Chlorina about to turn everyone's eyes red and make their skin itch?

"Hey, little dudes!"

Eugene looked up. It wasn't Queen Chlorina after all. It was Ted, the teenage lifeguard. His long blond hair reflected the sun like

aluminum foil. He wore a green Westville Swim Team tank top.

"There's no running around my pool." Lifeguard Ted pointed out the dangers of running: slipping, sliding, falling, bumping your head, breaking an arm or leg, chipping a tooth, stubbing a toe, falling into the pool, . . . and a whole lot more.

"And can you dudes be careful in the shallow end 'cause there are even littler dudes in the little dude part."

Clearly Ted had no idea about the evils of Scuba-Doobot. *If he*

knew the truth about what was at the bottom of the pool, he'd be running too, thought Eugene.

"Eugene!" Eugene's mother called him from the pool steps. The danger had not passed, for Eugene now faced the most awesome enemy of all time: Getting in Trouble with Mom!

"I thought I told you boys to behave at the pool!" Eugene's mom said. "Horsing around like that is dangerous!"

Eugene knew what that meant: no Super Dude Ice Poptacular to eat on the way home.

In a matter of minutes, the two dripping wet boys were semidry and sitting in the backseat of the car. It was a long, silent ride home. But it gave Eugene plenty of time to think.

That explains that lifeguard's Westville Swim Team tank top.

Lifeguard Ted must really be **the Double-Dipper**, a secret, spying double agent. That's just like a guy from Westville, thought Eugene.

That was when Eugene heard the blast of the Giant Whistle of Doom.

BREET-TWEET-TWEET!

Eugene and Charlie looked out the window. It was the sneaky Double-Dipper himself—half boy, half grown-up, all bad!

The Double-Dipper's greatest and sneakiest superpower was getting superheroes in trouble using his Tattletale Attack!

"You tattletaled on the wrong good guys, villain . . . ," Eugene said quietly.

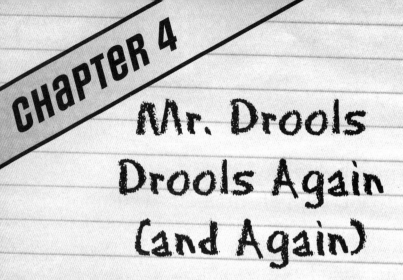

CHAPTER 4

Mr. Drools Drools Again (and Again)

By Eugene

"Chocolate chip cookies are the greatest thing since Super Dude No. 243!" Eugene said. His mouth was so stuffed, it really sounded like: "Chclt ch coos arf fee glate thin imf supf duf two fotty."

Charlie understood every word and said "Yeah!," but it sounded like "Ehhh" because his mouth was full of chocolate chip cookies too.

Eugene swallowed. "Your mom makes the best Cosmic Chip

Cookies in the universe!"

"Only the best for the Super-hero Squad's Weekly Sleepover Meeting!" Charlie stated, grabbing another cookie.

Stuffed full of cosmic goodness, Eugene and Charlie plotted out tomorrow's adventure. They were going back to the community pool to start swimming lessons.

"After we learn to dive like fish, evil won't be able to run, fly, or *swim* from the Sunnyview Super-hero Squad!" Eugene said.

Charlie's dad entered the bedroom carrying the Turbomobile with him. "Hi, boys. I mean, excuse the intrusion, heroes of Sunnyview," he said. Turbo was pressed against the plastic ball, squeaking at Charlie and Eugene. "Turbo rolled all the way to the TV room."

"Sorry, Dad," Charlie said.

"He might've heard some evil outside."

"No problem. Your mom wanted me to remind you that you left your swimsuits outside."

SWIMSUITS!

"Only one more day until swimming lessons begin!" Charlie shouted.

"MI-TEE!" Eugene shouted so loudly that Mr. Jones decided it was time to return to the TV room. He was getting used to hearing "MI-TEE!" around the house whenever Eugene was around.

Once Mr. Jones was gone, Eugene thought he heard a growl. Maybe Charlie's dad was playing a trick on them?

GRRR!

There it was again! Eugene knew that was no playful Dad-growl—it was the horrible, slobbery growl of—

"Mr. Drools!" Eugene shouted.

"He's back!" cried Charlie.

The swimsuits! Eugene thought immediately. *My Captain Awesome Swimming Battlesuit is hanging outside with Nacho Cheese Man's Cheddartrunks!*

Sometimes superheroes protected whole towns. Other times they protected people, but sometimes superheroes needed to protect their Swimming Battlesuits from the terrible slobber of Mr. Drools. No evil dog from the Howling Paw Nebula would ruin their swimming lessons!

CHAPTER 5

Everybody into the Pool!

By Eugene

"**W**hy look, it's Puke-Gene and his friend Barfy Jones."

UGH.

Eugene knew that voice could only belong to one person on the planet: Meredith Mooney.

So much for our Meredith-free summer, thought Eugene.

"Hello, My! Me! Mine! Mere-DITH!!" Eugene said, rolling his eyes.

Being Meredith, she was of course wearing a bright pink swim-suit and matching pink goggles.

"She probably has barfy pink flippers and a matching barfy pink kickboard in her mom's car," Charlie whispered to Eugene.

It was the first day of swim-ming lessons and Meredith wasn't

the only person from Eugene and Charlie's class who was learning to swim.

Sally Williams was there, too. And Bernie Melnik and Evan Mason. It was like a regular school day, except instead of homework there was water. And no desks because . . . they'd sink.

**BREET-
TWEET-
TWEET!**

Eugene knew that sound! It was the whistle of his old enemy Ted the Lifeguard, back to tattle a tale once more and make sure another kid wouldn't get his Super Dude Ice Poptacular!

"What ho, little dudes," he said. "Welcome to my swim class."

SHOCK!

GASP!

SHOCK AGAIN!

The Double-Dipper is our swim teacher?

Charlie nudged Eugene. This was badness without any goodness. "We're really going to have to watch this guy," Charlie whispered.

TWEET!

"Into the pool, swimmer dudes," Ted said.

SPLASH!

Once in the water the class hung on to the side of the pool and started kicking.

"That's the way, dudes," Ted said. "You're doing awesome." He even had a compliment for Mere-DITH. "Gnarly kick, dudette!"

Gnarly kick? Does the Double-Dipper not know that Meredith Mooney is secretly Little Miss Stinky Pinky, the grossest, pinkest villain in all the school systems in the universe and the galaxy?

The forces of good could never let stinky pink villains do better— even when it came to poolside kicking! On land, superheroes were fantastic, but in the water, they must be *splashtastic!*

Little Miss Stinky Pinky had to be splashed

before her show-offyness took total control of the swim class and turned everyone into stinky pink brain zombies.

PLUS! The Double-Dipper needed to know that Captain Awesome and Nacho Cheese Man were wise to his double agent ways.

Eugene and Charlie counted, "One, two, three . . . MI-TEE!" The boys kicked their feet like they were chasing Mr. Drools. Water splashed everywhere! They kicked faster!

SPLISH!

And faster!

SPLASH!

And faster!

SPLISH! SPLASH! SPLOSH!

Little Miss Stinky Pinky squealed like pink villains do when they get wet, and the Double-Dipper ran for cover. Evil is no match for the splashing might of the Superhero Squad!

"Charlie! Eugene! Out of the pool!" Ted yelled. "Not cool, dudes. Uncool!"

OOPS.

Eugene and Charlie climbed up from the pool.

I guess swimming lessons are over for today, thought Eugene.

"Dudes, why don't you chill with some dudely time-outs," Ted suggested.

Eugene and Charlie headed to the snack bar. They were sure to get double-dipped when Ted tattletaled to their moms that they were misbehaving at the pool again.

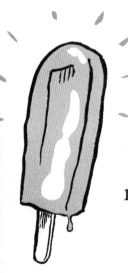

But evil had been stopped and covered in water!

"A Super Dude Ice Poptacular is just what we need!" Eugene said.

"Nothing more poptacular

after a hard day of splashing bad guys," Charlie agreed.

But the man behind the counter had a different idea.

"Why don't you boys have something healthier?" a familiar, evil voice threatened.

"YUCK!" the friends gasped.

That's right! Dr. Yuck Spinach, the evil cackling chef from Sunnyview Elementary cafeteria was

now working at the pool's snack shop!

That's what he was doing after school; he was getting ready to serve his awful vegetable surprises to all the summer swimmers. He was even wearing his hairnet. Looks like evil had a part-time summer job!

But no one wants to eat peas or zucchini in the summer!

On a hot day!

At. The. Pool!

DOUBLE YUCK!

If the evil Dr. Spinach wouldn't serve Super Dude Ice Poptaculars to Eugene and Charlie, maybe he'd hand them over to Captain Awesome and Nacho Cheese Man. . . .

CHAPTER 6

The Blob-Blob of Blobbiness

By Eugene

"Okay, little swimmers! Give your swim buddy a high five for a job well done!" Ted called out at the end of the next day's lesson. "Class is over, so enjoy some pool time until your parental units arrive."

Eugene gave Charlie a high five. "Not waves nor chlorine nor

public swimming pool pee-pee will keep us from our goal of becoming the best swimmers in the universe. Those were some MI-TEE kicks you did, Charlie."

"You too, Eugene," Charlie replied. "I think we earned some floating time in the shallow end."

Unfortunately, there were only two pool noodles. One was blue and the other was—*GASP!*—PINK and looked like Mr. Drools had been chewing on it.

"*You* take the blue, Charlie. You earned it," Eugene insisted.

"Are you sure, Eugene? We could just sit on the steps."

"No one said being a superhero would be easy," Eugene reminded his best friend. "Sometimes in the battle for goodness you just gotta take the pink noodle floatie."

Eugene jumped back into the pool and lay across his pink floatie. The water was warm, the sun was warmer, and the young superhero

had nothing to do but breathe. There were only two words for a day like that.

"MI-TEE . . ." Eugene sighed.

Actually, it was really only one word, but Eugene was a superhero, able to do super things . . . like make one word sound like two.

"Oh, look at the two little babies, floating in the shallow end like scaredy-babies crying for their mommies!" Meredith's annoying voice shouted from across the pool.

Charlie sat up and looked around. "Who let BABIES in the pool?!"

Eugene didn't answer. He knew very well whom Meredith was calling a baby. The fact that he had chosen the pink noodle floatie didn't help. Eugene expected to see Meredith playing in the water next to them. He looked up and that's when he saw SHE WAS IN THE DEEP END!

"Stay calm. Make no sudden moves," Eugene whispered. "Charlie, this just got serious."

"What's wrong? You afraid there's a big, bad monster in the deep end?" Meredith taunted. "Why don't you two just stay down there and splash with the other babies?"

"We can't let her talk to us like that!" Charlie said.

"Of course not," Eugene said. "She's given me a great idea."

SLAPPP!

Eugene and Charlie slapped their hands in the water as hard as they could.

A big wave of water rolled across the pool and splashed Meredith.

BULLSEYE!

Her pinkest pink ribbons washed out of her hair. There was nothing Meredith could do now, so she stuck out her tongue.

Eugene felt so good about their splashy victory over Meredith that it didn't seem so bad that he was floating around the pool on the pink noodle that kept sinking.

But then he saw IT!

A . . .

Strange . . .

BLOB!

And it waited silently—as most

blobs do—at the **VERY BOTTOM OF THE DEEP END!** If this were a monster movie, scary music would be blasting! People would be screaming! Panic would spread across the planet!

Eugene didn't move a muscle.

"Stay calm. Make no sudden moves," Eugene whispered. "Charlie, this just got serious."

"Not again!" Charlie gasped.

"This time . . . even more," Eugene whispered.

"EVEN MORE?!" Charlie gasped louder. "Wait. Even more than what?"

"Even more than last time it was serious!" Eugene warned.

"Wow. That *is* serious."

"On the count of three, I want you to panic as loudly as you can and swim like the Jelly Squirrels from Super Dude No. 32," Eugene quietly explained, afraid to take his eyes off the mysterious blob down below.

"One . . . two . . ."

"Panic like a Jelly Squirrel!"

Charlie screamed and, well, pan-icked exactly like a Jelly Squirrel.

Charlie's panic made Eugene panic! Eugene's panic made Charlie panic even more! And Charlie's even-more panic made Eugene panic even double-more!

Sink?! That is *not* a word you want to hear on your second day of swimming lessons! And probably not even on your *third* day, either!

Eugene slipped from his floatie.

His arms slapped at the water. His legs kicked hard, waiting for the Blobby Blob-Blob from the Deep End to grab him by the ankles.

"Hold on little dude!" Ted shouted and raced toward Eugene.

And then, like an ice cream sundae with a cherry on top arriving to save

the day after
a big plate of
boiled carrots, a hand
appeared before Eugene's
face.

"Grab my hand!" the voice shouted.

Eugene didn't need to be told twice. He grabbed the hand and pulled himself safely to the edge of the pool.

"Thanks," Eugene gasped.

"No worries, Eugene," a voice

replied. Eugene froze. It wasn't Ted's voice. It was a *girl's*.

The pool water cleared from Eugene's eyes and he realized he was holding Sally Williams's hand.

Oh man! The only thing worse

than being saved by a girl is holding her hand afterward!

GIRL HAND! BLECH!

Eugene yanked his hand back.

"I guess we're kinda equal now since you found Mr. Whiskersworth for me."

"Yeah. I guess."

Eugene's replies were limited to as few words as possible. His face was redder than the Human Tomato's *Atsa Lotsa Pasta Sauce* that Super Dude always bought from his local grocer.

"Whoa! Are you okay, little

dude?" Ted asked, rushing over to Eugene and Sally.

Eugene nodded.

"Rad save, Sally!" Ted smiled to Sally and gave her a high five.

"Don't worry, Ted. I do this kind of thing all the time." Sally

smiled and high-fived him.

Eugene raised an eyebrow and snapped a look to Sally. Eugene wasn't sure if Sally meant that she-saved people all the time or gave high fives.

The thought of Sally as a hero was a strange one, but it wasn't the strangest thing of all. Who sent the evil Blobby Blob-Blob from the Deep End to blob Eugene?

CHAPTER 7

Welcome to Stinkopia

By Eugene

"**O**kay, little swimmers! Today you little dudes and dudettes get to take turns diving off the side of the pool," Ted announced.

"Isn't it too shallow here?" Meredith asked.

"Confirm-o-mento, Mere," Ted replied. "And that's why we'll be jumping into the pool **in the deep end!**"

The kids cheered! The kids splashed! The kids high-fived! Well, all the kids but *one* to be exact.

"IN THE DEEP END!"
"IN THE DEEP END!"
"IN THE DEEP END!"

The words echoed over and over

in Eugene's head like a broken parrot robot. The thought of going back to the deep end gave Eugene a funny twisting in his stomach, even worse than the time he snuck some of Charlie's spicy jalapeño cheese.

The other kids in swim class climbed from the pool and walked to the far side. Didn't they know that the Blobby Blob-Blob from the Deep End might still be down there waiting to blob them!?

Eugene climbed from the pool and tugged on Ted's hand.

"What's up, Dude-gene?" Ted asked.

"I . . . um . . . I . . . need to go to the bathroom!"Eugene was already racing away before the last word left his mouth.

Eugene ran into the boy's bathroom and locked himself in one of the bathroom stalls.

It's no big deal, Eugene thought. *I'm sure Super Dude locked himself in a bathroom before.*

Eugene tried to calm himself. He inhaled deeply.

PEE-YEW!

Bad idea! Eugene was in a stinky bathroom!

"Come on, Eugene!" he said to himself. "Instead of hiding here in Stinkopia, you should be out fighting the Blobby Blob-Blob from the Deep End! Who knows what blobby

I.P. FREELY WAS HERE.

blobness that blob will be blobbing on everyone!"

"Stand back, villain, or else prepare to be cheesed by Nacho Cheese Man!" Charlie rushed into the bathroom, dripping wet and blasting cheese. But instead of seeing Eugene trapped by a villainous villain, Charlie was met by an empty bathroom now covered in cheese.

"Aw, man. What a waste of good cheese," Charlie sighed, then added, "You in here Eugene?"

"Over here," Eugene called out from the stall.

"I knew it!" Charlie shouted. "Were you attacked by the Toilet of Terror? Hold on! I'll save you from its Flush of Fear!

"I'm fine," Eugene lied. "It's just ... I think I ate one too many Super Dude Ice Poptaculars, that's all."

"Oh," Charlie said, disappointed his friend wasn't stuck in an evil toilet, fighting against the Flush of Fear. "You've been gone for like a jillion minutes. Ted said you're going to miss your turn to dive . . ."

"Um . . . yeah. Can you tell him that's okay? Maybe next time?"

Eugene sat quietly and listened

to Charlie leave. The twisting in his stomach was replaced with a dull ache—one that seemed to wrap itself around his heart.

That *had* to be it, right? One too many Super Dude Ice Poptaculars? After all, superheroes like Super Dude don't get scared.

But, maybe, their secret identities do. . . .

CHAPTER 8

Turbo to the Rescue!

By
Eugene

No matter how Eugene twisted, turned, or moved, he couldn't fall asleep. How could he? Tomorrow was Friday.

Isn't Friday the most awesomest of awesome days? Even during summer vacation Friday was like the best parts of Monday, Tuesday, Wednesday, and Thursday all rolled up into one day called Monuesnesursday. It was pizza day at school and THE night for Sunnyview Superhero Squad Sleepovers.

BUT!

This Friday meant something else. It was the last day of Eugene's swim lessons. Eugene would have to jump off the diving board and into . . . *the deep end.*

Eugene couldn't remember the last time he felt this unawesome, but it probably involved his mom and the words "vegetables," "no," and "dessert."

Eugene plopped back onto his bed and covered his face with his pillow.

"Blah!" he groaned.

Turbo raced on his squeaky

wheel, getting his little muscles ready for their next mission. Eugene sat up and stared at his sidekick. Turbo stopped running. He looked right at Eugene and said, "Squeak! Squeak!"

"You're right, Turbo! We have to be brave! That's what superheroes do!" Eugene climbed from his bed. He clenched his fists and puffed out his chest, because heroic moments like this required chest-puffing.

"It's our job to protect the Sunnyview Community Pool from the Blobby Blob-Blob from the Deep End! And no blobby blob-blob is gonna stop me from doing it!"

It was here . . . the last day of swim class!

With a newfound courage in his heart (Eugene had thanked Turbo for the pep talk the night before), Eugene arrived at the pool ready for action.

"Try not to get sick on Super Dude Ice Poptaculars today, Eugenio!" Meredith giggled.

Eugene ignored Meredith. For one, she looked pinker than cotton candy with pigtails, and for two, Eugene was on a mission.

"Okay, C-man!" Ted said to Charlie. "You get to go for the big dive first!"

Charlie gave a quick smile and thumbs-up to Eugene. Everyone was watching Charlie, so Eugene took two slow, silent steps

away from the group, then raced
toward the locker room.

Charlie stopped at the end
of the diving board and looked
into the water below. There was
something in the pool! Something . . .

BLOBBY!

"Go ahead, C-Man!
I've got you covered!"
Ted called up to him.

"But there's something in the pool," Charlie replied.

"I'm here for you, Nacho Cheese Man!" Captain Awesome shouted as he rushed to the diving board. Captain Awesome threw a can of cheese and Charlie snagged it in midair.

"What are you *doing*, Eugene?" Charlie whispered once Captain Awesome joined him.

"Saving you from Little Miss Stinky Pinky's Blobby Blob-Blob!"

And with those brave words,

Captain Awesome dove into the water!

"MI-TEEEEEEEEEEE!"

"Whoa," a stunned Ted said, then turned to the other kids and asked, "Who's Nacho Cheese Man?"

Under water, Captain Awesome dove to the bottom to battle with the Blobby Blob-Blob from the Deep.

The Blobby Blob-Blob squirmed and wormed, but Captain Awesome would not let it go. He burst to the surface, the dreaded creature firmly clenched in his superhands.

"Not all your blobbiness shall save you from my awesome grip of goodness!" Captain Awesome said as he wrestled the creature.

"Hold on, Captain Awesome!" Charlie called out from above and dove into the water. A can of nacho cheese squirted wildly in his hand.

"Whoa," a stunned Ted said, then turned to the other kids and asked, "Who's Captain Awesome?"

CHAPTER 10

Badness Always Loses

By Eugene

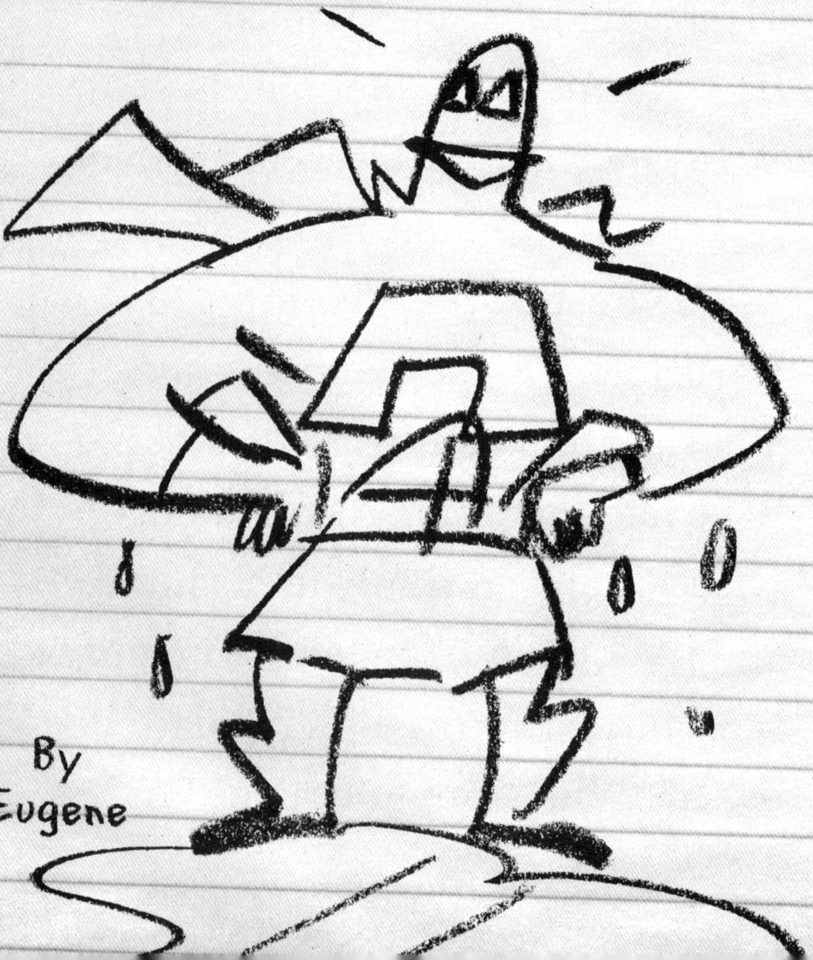

"Thanks for the save, Captain Awesome. I don't know what would've happened if I jumped off that diving board without you there to help me." Charlie stuck the can of cheese in his mouth and gave a suck, then offered it to Captain Awesome. "Want some?"

But Captain Awesome had more on his mind than cheese. The Blobby Blob-Blob from the Deep

End lay on the ground, looking less blobby and evil than it had before getting Captain Awesome's 1-2 Underwater Punch.

"Look!" Captain Awesome gasped. "The Blobby Blob-Blob looks like a green giraffe!"

"I always knew giraffes were evil!" Charlie said, hitting his palm with his fist.

But it wasn't just an evil giraffe. It was Eugene's baby sister Molly's deflated giraffe floatie! It had popped and sunk to the bottom of the pool!

"Gah! Goo! Garggelsnansjboo!"

"By all that's gibberish!" cried Captain Awesome at hearing the babbling of his most arch-of-enemies. "Could it be true?! Queen Stinkypants from the Planet Baby teamed up with Little Miss Stinky Pinky?!"

It *was* true! For there sat Queen Stinkypants in a lounge chair right next to Eugene's mom! She was smelly! She was stinky! She was sticky!

Sticky?!

"ARRRRRRRRRR! She's eating my Super Dude Ice Poptacular!" Captain Awesome groaned. "Her terrible trick worked! Why didn't we see her stinky stink was the real evil behind this plot?"

"Because you can't smell evil underwater, C.A. Even stinky evil," Charlie reminded him.

The Super Dude Ice Poptacular may have been lost, but Little Miss Stinky Pinky and Queen Stinkypants were defeated! Captain Awesome's awesome work was done. The Blobby Blob-Blob was defeated and would blobby blob-blob little swimmers no more!

"That was one cool-a-mundo dive, dude," Ted said to Captain Awesome. "But next time, no super-hero costumes allowed in the pool. It's not safe to swim in a cape."

Eugene nodded because super-heroes had to follow the rules.

"I return the pool to your watch-ful eye, Ted," Captain Awesome said. "Continue your fight against sunburn, swimming too soon after you eat, and running by the pool!"

"Will do, little dude, and don't worry, 'Badness always loses.'"

Did Ted *really* just say Super

Dude's favorite saying?! Ted gave a wink and Captain Awesome knew he was leaving the pool in safe hands. Perhaps Ted was not the tattletale double-agent spy, the Double-Dipper, after all! No fan of Super Dude could ever be anything but awesome.

Captain Awesome smiled before

racing back to the locker room.

"That was one cool little super-dude," Ted said.

★ ★ ★ ★ ★

The day was done, but even more importantly,

swim class was done. Everyone got Ted's "Excellent Swimmer" medals because they were all excellent little swimmers. Eugene took home the best prize of all: Swim Teacher Ted's Best of All High Dive Award.

Eugene's awesome dive as Captain Awesome had earned him

the top honor in his class! That was way better than Meredith's Safest Swimmer Award or Charlie's Most Improved Paddler.

Eugene and Charlie offered a quick wave good-bye. There was no need for anything more, for they'd soon be seeing each other again at the Superhero Squad Sleepover.

It was Friday, after all.

Eugene slid into the backseat of his mom's car. With a quick click of the seat belt, he was safe, secure, and ready to go home. Molly was already in her car seat,

gnawing away at some poor doll's
head.

　　Eugene felt happy. He sat back
and closed his eyes. Bad guys,
beware! Captain Awesome and

Nacho Cheese Man had once again made Sunnyview safe! No villain was too bad! No pool was too deep! No Blobby Blob-Blob was too blobby!

Only one thing could make this day even more perfect . . .

Eugene's mom closed her door, then reached between the seats and handed something to her son.

"I got you another Super Dude Ice Poptacular since Molly ate yours . . ."

Eugene took the sugary treat and smiled.

MI-TEE!

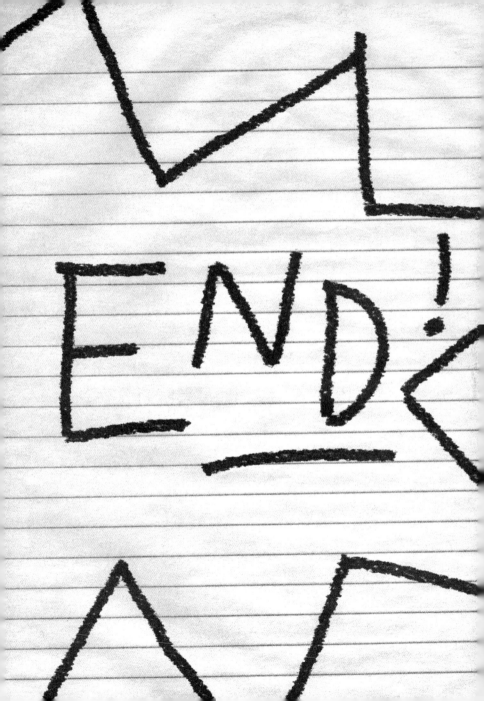

COMING
NEXT:

Keep reading
for a sneak peek at the next
CAPTAIN AWESOME
adventure!

No. 5

CAPTAIN AWESOME, SOCCER STAR

Fall. Who names a season after an accident? Are there other seasons called "Trip" or "Crash" or "Oops"?

NO.

So why name it "fall"?

Whatever the reason, it was certainly better than "Autumn." *I'll bet no one even knows what that word means,* Eugene thought.

Fall was the most boring, BORING, BO-RING time of year between the start of the school year and winter break—a time when NOTHING happens.

Oh sure, you can say that there's

Halloween, but that's *really* only for one day and sometimes it rains. Thanksgiving? What really happens on Thanksgiving besides a lot of eating, falling asleep in front of the television and having to listen to wrinkly old relatives say, "Oh, my! Look how big so-and-so has gotten!"

KA-THUNKK!

"OUCH!" cried Eugene, his thoughts now focused on things hitting his head.

I'm under attack! Eugene thought and dove for cover behind a tree. *But who could it be?!*